Here lies the first page of your regrettable endeavor into the histories of three inquisitive children who meet their end at various moments of life as the cause of particularily specific and so much so unoriginal entrapments and basic situations in which we all find one day or another, a life, or perhaps as some would rather or yet better feel to call it – what is a path to an inevitable grave.

Also by Micah Genest

The Land of Ick and Eck: Harlot's Encounters

Micah Genest

Three Stories About Children Who Die

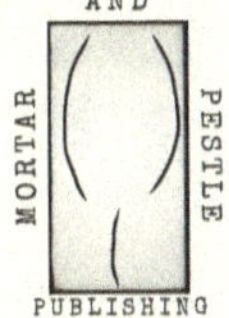

First Printing 2018

Printed Somewhere

For permission rights, contact the publisher at the address below:

mortarandpestlepublishing.com
info@mortarandpestlepublishing.com

Caution: This is a work of fiction. Though names, characters, incidents, situations, or other may sound familiar, they are products of the author's imagination, simply used in a fictitious manner. Any resemblance to actual persons, or realities, which there definitely are, either that be of persons living or dead, or perhaps of passed or of future events, they are to be understood as purely "coincidental," for that is the life we have agreed on, is it not? Thus, it is to be said, these are a simple parade of unforeseen happenings in which we agree to never have seen.

Mortar and Pestle Publishing
ISBN 978-1-7753721-2-7

While the reader May Be Preparing Themselves For An Ending That Will Surely Satisfy their Peculiar, Per Say, and So So Refined Taste, I Do Have To Warn That they Are Most Likely Too Dull To Be Able To Fully Appreciate The Magnificence That Stands Before them. Nevertheless, Here Follows The Final Chapter Of This Story. Chapter, The Finale. En Petite.

- Chapter: Untitled
  - Section I: A Forsaken Continuation
  - Section II: A Clown
  - Section III: The Parable
  - Section IV: A Reaction Of Sensibility
  - Section V: Of The Snakes
  - Section VI: Hate
  - Section VII: Love

this book is dedicated to absolutely no one

The First Story of This Book About a Child Who Dies

The Island of Gruel

A Story of a Stone-Pair Girl

And

The Myriads of Shintar Rock

A Necessary Introduction

Not too far from somewhere, there was a place of sea fairing folk, where the auspicious people dosed themselves with a sacredness called gruel; they believed the fine mush to be some sort of marvel, given to them by the Myriads of Shintar Rock. The Stone-Pairs, as they named themselves, would mix the gruel in their grog, and in their beds, and in their soups, and in their shoes, and even stuff the stuff inside of fish and shellfish, before being cooked and after when in their mouths. Some would leave the gruel on rocks and wait until the sun would turn it, then soak the pile with fresh water everyday, letting it drip and drip, away and away, until nothing but rock was left. Others plastered the wonder around the base of young saplings; nothing more, nothing less.

However, the Myriads of Shintar Rock denied ever giving these people gruel. As a matter of fact, the Myriads of Shintar Rock hated gruel. They thought it to be the most despicable concoction ever created.

In any event, the sea fairing folk never went a long moment without worshiping the gruel and thanking the Myriads of Shintar Rock for bringing it to them.

Part I

HOPE IN THE SHAPE OF A HOARSE VOICE

On an eve, a girl named Elizabeth found herself mixing a large barrel of the mentioned substance for her father.

"Old man," muttered the girl, "I believe your gruel is done."

The hoary weather worn face grimaced at Elizabeth, with his routine bulging red eyes, as he was on due with his seventh goblet of grog-gruel that day. Without a word, he flicked his fingers, signaling the girl to keep on stirring until he decided it was ready and time to stop.

Elizabeth bowed her head and continued on with her task.

"Oh rhmm…gruel," mumbled the old man. "Whadever would-I do withou-ue?"

The father of the house was a noble man, the courageous respectable sort. He had the girl build him a rock throne, one fancy enough that anyone who saw it would be jealous (not that anyone else did see it). The throne was six feet high and six feet wide (a perfect size to be put six feet deep). The man used to make a hefty profit-selling eels stuffed with gruel, as they were quite the delicacy for the Stone-Pairs. However, the genteel father eventually lost interest in anything other than his marvelous aged gruel, and thus stayed inside his ostentatious shack, during day, during night, making sure his daughter continued on with her stirring.

"Keep'ms string," slurred the old man.

And so the girl continued on, singing sorrowfully inside her head as she did:

If ever I was, I was not me,
I would cast a sail with harmony.

I would search to the ends
To the ends of the sea,
And the wind and the winds
Would all carry me.

Out and cast.
Out at last.
Out I'd go,
Fast! Fast! Fast!

But Elizabeth was she, and she was in a dismal place, downcast, like a fish that had no hope to taste the sea. She was doomed to stir for her father. Doomed to stir for her father. Doomed to stir for her father.

This was the story that continued on for longer than the reader would be able to bear to know, until the girl heard a hoarse voice for the umpteenth time.

"My child," were the words heeded to.

"Miss," responded Elizabeth. "Where are you?"

"Look below child," was the answer. "I am always below."

And sure enough, in the barrel of gruel below, there the hoarse voiced woman was. The girl was ever so pleased to see her friend; she had not seen her for some time.

"Where have you been?" asked Elizabeth.

"Never mind that," uttered the hoarse-voiced-woman in haste. "Now, listen. In a fortnight, when the moon shows its face, when your hands are no longer numb, you shall cut off the head from that wicked old man."

Part II

A COUNTERINTUITIVE TRADITION

Shintar Rock had never been seen by any eye of the Stone-Pair people; it was more of lore than something proven by the expertise of scientific witnesses, or definite proven empirical thoughts of undeniable and unchangeable reality.

Yet, it existed.

And it was a grand place, grand indeed, with mountains full of trees, and trees full of leaves, where birds needed walking sticks if they ever wished to make themselves from one side of the land to the next, and where turtles needed handkerchiefs to glide from one stone to another. Shintar Rock was a place covered in water, lots and lots of water, but not completely. There was just enough for the Myriads to travel about with ease, which they did on little boats made of nutshells and wetted paper pulp, accompanied by diamond shaped sponge sails. Some boats were built with exceptionally captivating oars, very much like ivory piano keys with little people dancing on them; each were leveled and carved with superb precision and dexterity, while others even more.

The Stone-Pairs had stories about Shintar Rock and the Myriads who resided within. Some of these tales told how, near the beginning of time, when humans were starving, having nothing to eat but each other, the Myriads came to the Stone-Pairs with gruel, as if from the heavens unto their salvation, like a cornucopia, gathered from the fields of the gods. No longer were the Stone-Pairs to be cursed to eat the tender ribs of their vulnerable newborns, or the newly ripened thighs of the naive youths, or the lean calves of their feeble elders. From then on, they could populate and grow as a liberal people, eventually to become masters over their lands and others, cracking their shackles, their anchor, their tackles, reeling with hooks, wherever they so desired.

Another tale told of how, when a great fog of darkness covered the earth, the Myriads came down from the heavens onto Shintar Rock, where they worked in great labour, collecting flames, ices, muds, and airs. Only after the purest of each had been found, the elements were combined, and a great light was produced. And out of that light came gruel, which the Myriads brought to the Stone-Pairs, who were from that day, to the next, and forever, blessed, no longer to be in the darkness of the fog, but to bask in the light of gruel.

Yet, in accordance to their description, the Myriads were more like swarming ants glued to a pool of honey than gods. They were small, intricately designed, each included with two stone boots, a pair of large cotton trousers, an oval hat, and a blubbery off-white upper body.

There existed a dozen in total. By the time of this story, four had died; thus, eight were left.

And, if one were to enter into the Myriads's history at the time of the mentioned Elizabeth, they would find themselves witnessing a strange sight indeed.

It was on an eve that the Myriads had dutifully collected the strongest and thinnest of vines they could find. The vines had to be of the trustworthy sort, for they were for the making of nooses for the Gallows Ritual.

You see, every decided time, the Myriads would sacrifice one of their own in order to have one less. It was a crucial part of their culture, as it identified them as a unique identity of one, an abiding community, and a race of inseparable collaborators of alliance.

None of them were particularly fond of being hanged, but it was tradition.

The sacrifice was chosen by engaging in a heated rivalry to the center of the sacred mountain, Mount Wet-Oat. The mountain was filled with trials of every sort, such as rain-storms, snow-storms, wind-storms, cloud-storms, earth-storms, dust-storms; sometimes there were even molten-storms and amber-storms. If one so happened to defeat all others, and made themselves into the heart of Mount Wet-Oat, the winner would have the privilege to pay homage and display the sacred custom of the Myriads.

And so, when the last of the nooses were constructed for the hanging, the Myriads began their assessment: each took a knife, made a hole in the palm of a rock, placed the opposite side of the knot through the hole, tied it firmly, then threw the noose towards the sea. It took several throws for some to touch the water, being poor casters. Eventually, with great determination, they all succeeded, and then waited in silence, watching as skeleton like whales leap above the still waters, screeching unpleasant high-pitched noises, collapsing into piles of debris upon the sea tops, ruminants quickly consumed by passerby scavengers, until the first noose made its way back in the mouth of an eel.

The competition to Mount Wet-Oat had begun.

Part III

THE DEED DONE AND TRICKLES OF FREEDOM

When Elizabeth awoke the morning of the task, she waited in her room, pressing her numb fingers to her ears, making sure she heard nothing. Nothing would stop the night from coming.

Nothing at all.

Though her father cursed on his throne throughout the day, screaming for the gruel to be stirred, the girl did not move, hidden in another room.

The night was to come.

And at last the night came.

"Stir the gruel you happy girl of mine," soberly demanded the father when Elizabeth had made herself before him. "I should put you in a well and fill it with rocks. I should. I will. Get yourself over here. I'll be…"

"Do it now," called out the hoarse-voiced-woman.

"But how?" questioned Elizabeth.

The father looked over his shoulder, confused, then shouted with more displeasure, "Get on with your stirring. Too much time wasted already."

"Do it," repeated the hoarse-voiced-woman.

Though the girl had been set on cutting off the old man's head, she had forgotten to think about how she would do it. Thoughts of opening the front door of her father's home and making herself away had replayed again and again in her head, but the manner in which she would achieve her freedom had somehow become secondary, than third, then forgotten altogether within the world of her mind.

"Do it now!" cried out the hoarse-voiced-woman again.

So, in a heartened and unplanned manner, Elizabeth took hold of a neglected blade her father had used for his eels some long time ago, and made her way through the neck with determination. It was a laborious process, as bone is quite difficult to separate; but eventually, with much effort and messiness, only a scant worth of flesh was left to cut at one moment, and then the head finally fell off entirely at the next.

"You are free!" rejoiced the hoarse-voiced-woman from the spreading pond of redness upon the floor. "You must get away from this place. Take what ever you can that is useful."

It is quite true that the girl felt proud of herself for accomplishing the task, though she stayed focused on her new undertaking, careful not to become too nostalgic. She collected her favorite pale and blanket, and as if second nature filled said items with gruel. When finished, she took her feet and placed them and herself in front of a door that led to the outside world.

Yet, Elizabeth was hesitant at first; she was not sure if her father would let her leave.

"Go now!" persisted the hoarse-voiced-woman.

The girl pressed herself forward, slowly at first, but then with a freeing feeling, she sped forth with a swift quickness, raising her flailing hands above her head, squealing all the way to the edge of the sea.

It was brilliant.

She ran and screamed with utter joy. If the moment would have been let to continue, Elizabeth would have galloped along the entire shoreline, teasing the rising waves, every single inch that wished to cross her paddling feet.

But, with a sudden force, a great wind from the eastern harbors blew; the girl was thrashed inside of a delicate, large boat made of fading barnacles.

After hitting her head on the thwart, a darkness came over her.

Part IV

AN INEVITABLE DEMISE

Though unknown to the general populace, or any population for that matter, may they be clever or obtuse, Myriads were quite known for their passionate gorging in muscatels. Also, though unorthodox, they preferred to eat them prior to any sort of drying, for they believed that parched looking objects are simply ghastly, deserving the fate of trite or quaint things. However wholesome, there was no place for the old and exposed; only the new were pleasant to look at.

Thus, it is to be expected, that once the eight witnessed the arrival of the final noose, they all partook in a great feast of muscatels, celebrating that each of their nooses were worthy of hanging one of them when the sacred time came to be.

So they ate and ate and ate, indulging in their gluttonous dinner fabulously, intrepidly filling mouths and stomachs to the greatest of limits, risking the ripping and bursting of their blubbery bodies, each like a fat dam maliciously irritated by an outburst of a league of decanting clouds.

At the end of the feast, after all were content, they slept.

When morning came, the day that marked the laborious and dangerous journey up Mount Wet-Oat, only six of the Myriads woke: two were dead, while the others felt horribly sick.

There believed to have been a poisoning.

Inevitably, with hard work and determination, a loud confusion develop as each claimed with honourable rhetoric that it was them or they who had poisoned them all somehow. The hectic ensemble of arguments continued for some time, climaxing with fingers being pointed into every direction, as if all were conductors and each proclaimed to hold the authoritative baton. In the end, the Myriads came to the consensus that the sacred Trial of Gruel, which had never been preformed before, as they all hated what it entailed, would be conducted at that time, so that they may go on and finish the Gallows Ritual.

As you will soon notice, after shaking your head at the repetitive nature of the Myriads overuse of proscribed procedures, I have strategically waited until this point to speak of the their detailed relationship with gruel, as this strategy has been advantageous for narrative purposes, or something like that.

Hence the following: it is true that the Myriads hated gruel; in fact, they despised it as if it would be the source of their preordained demise. Nevertheless, gruel-trees did grow on Shintar Rock, and they were notoriously impossible to eradicate, meaning, the Myriads were continually forced to cope with the hated substance.

In primeval days, in order to get rid of the gruel, large barnacle boats, much larger and sturdier than those used to get about the island, were brimmed with gruel-trees. When full, the boats would be delivered unto the sea to be taken far, far away from them. However, the tactic was terribly inefficient, for the gruel-trees grew back to their full mature heights within a few days, and the boats themselves took months to build, for the Myriads only used goose barnacles, and according to those welching cave hermits, especially the ones who would catch urchins for cooking in the dead of night, say that one can only obtain such crustaceans on driftwood, and so that is the only place that the Myriads looked for them.

When modern times came, due to the influence of dwindling numbers of the Myriads, the gruel-trees were simply set on fire and allowed to burn all year round. Though much of the gruel, which manifested in ball form, was devoured in the bowels of the flames, rising towards the skies in great streaks of red smoke, the gruel only burnt when ready to eat, acting like a paradoxical oven. Curiously, the fire did not burn away any bark, branches, leaves, twigs, flowers, or any unripe gruel upon the trees, only the ripe gruel. Therefore, no matter how much effort was made, there has been, is, and will always be gruel on the Island of Shintar Rock.

For these reasons, it was possible for the Myriads to have a Trial of Gruel.

Now, for another explanation: A Trial of Gruel is when someone puts a gruel-ball into their mouth and successfully swallows it without choking; whoever can do so successfully is not guilty of whatever accusation that may have been placed upon them.

After paddling themselves in their little boats to a gruel-tree, the Myriads dowsed it with water to put out the flames, plucked six fully ripened gruel balls, and then all at once placed the gruel into their mouths.

And then they all choked.

Part V

TOWARDS AN UNKNOWN DESTINATION

Though Elizabeth's head throbbed when she awoke, she felt pleased at her overall situation. The weather was nice and the boat itself was quite accommodating, as it had a decent sized fireplace to keep her warm, a pile of straw to keep her comfortable, and many, many matches to keep her well occupied. The girl was delighted at the latter, for she liked lighting things on fire. Although there were no sails (as mentioned) or other things of the sort in the boat, such materials would have been quite useless, for Elizabeth did not know where she was or which direction anything could be. Thus, she went wherever the water decided, enjoying her newfound situation.

Not long after the girl fashioned a little fire in the fireplace, high above the boat, somewhere in the firmament, an overtly cinematic display of clouds began to take place. Though the sky looked welcoming a few moments ago, it quickly filled with visible masses of misty grey waters, which curdled and meshed themselves together, constricting one another like piles of dirty wet rags in an empty basin. Then rain fell.

Elizabeth had never felt rain before, only seen.

"No no no!" she exclaimed. "What are you doing to my fire? That's my fire, not yours."

Soon enough, the droplets of water quenched the flames; satisfied, they let out a latent stream of smoke.

The girl became quite nervous because of this, and of the dripping waters around her. The only possible solution that made sense was to eat gruel. And so she did. She scraped every morsel of gruel off of her blanket, as if suffering from an exemplary famine, eating with an unquenchable appetite. This process was repeated for the pale of gruel as well. Yet, sooner than the girl would have liked, all had become consumed.

"No no no!" cried Elizabeth.

The situation was disastrously stressful.

To add to her misery, the vast clouds continued to press together in their infinite wisdom and unforgiving calamity, deepening the absence of light, joined by vulgar shattering noises and bright needle like lights. And the rain was of the same mind; it fell with an even greater desire to wet the earth and fill the sea beyond content.

As the girl sat in the boat, without any fire or any gruel, she took more notice of the water that began to fall past her face and down her sides; while it was cold, the rain was like a tonic, comforting, invigorating. The drips made themselves around her, and made the situation very pleasing.

"I like rain," voiced the girl to herself, grateful.

Though Elizabeth was stuck in perhaps the exact middle of a sea, without any sight of shore around her; though the darkness of the clouds brought on an uncountable number of water drops that slowly filled the boat; though her pleasant fire had been extinguished; though she had no more gruel to occupy her mind; like a naturalist, she felt pleased before the mercy of Nature, for she was safer than she had ever been. So she sauntered forward within the boat, like an Irish monk, letting the sea take her wherever it may. Towards a new life. At last to fruition.

Eventually, the storm abated.

Surely enough, as due to accepted scientific principles and the laws of the gods, the water, which had accumulated itself within the boat, evaporated in approbation to the vacating clouds throughout the sky.

And then there was a great tug on the boat and a continuation of movement.

"What could that be?" exclaimed the girl, baffled; luckily, she had been seated when the sudden movement had occurred, for if she had been standing, she would have certainly fallen and hit her head again, perhaps to stay forever in the darkness this time. But that did not happen.

"My goodness," added Elizabeth, as she witnessed the seawater briskly rippling away from the sides of the boat, caused by some presently unknown force.

The girl tried to comprehend the situation in its entirety, pressing her fingers to her head. To observe every detail was now crucial for the collection of evidence, which would all have to be scrutinized without biases in order to achieve an objective opinion. With such a mindset, Elizabeth noticed in the direction the boat was being directed to, a poorly developed but colourful fin shimmering with psychedelic colours; it seemed to be struggling with much determination. After coming to the conclusion that it must be a living creature, the girl looked for the things head. When she found it, which supported her hypothesis, Elizabeth then saw that the things mouth contained a rock with a rope tied through its middle, and on the other end of the rope was a noose, which had become caught on the keel of the boat.

"Ha hah!" announced the girl; she had deducted that the cause of the moving boat was due to an eel.

Nevertheless, she was still ignorant to where the creature was headed to.

With further observation and contemplation, Elizabeth noticed, in the direction she, the boat, and the eel were headed, were long streams of red smoke rising up towards the sky, which came from what looked to be an mountainous island filled with bundles of flames and torrents of streams. The girl became quite stimulated at the sight of all this, for she believed she was headed towards an island made of fire and water.

Part VI

THE ISLAND OF GRUEL

The closer Elizabeth's eyes made themselves to the island, the more she began to shiver with delight: Red streaks of smoke. Un-consuming fires. And to her nose came a familiar and invigorating scent, gruel, which was well sharpened when the finned creature reached the island's edge, meeting with the seven other noose-carrying eels.

"This is all so eventful," shouted Elizabeth out loud. "There must be a great festival going on for the need of so many nooses."

But when the girl glided her eyes about, there was stillness; and when she peaked her ears for sounds, there was quietness. To add to her dismay, the boat she had been traveling upon went no further; it simply docked itself in the presence of the eels.

"Oh how unfortunate," voiced Elizabeth. "At least it looks comfortable were it is."

After taking hold of her blanket, pale, and matches, the girl put her feet onto scant patches of dry land and then began to search for something that would allow her to continue on.

(You see, there were countless of stringed waterways leading further into the island's depths, but the boat that had harbored Elizabeth was far too wide to make its way through any of them. And though the rational voices in our heads might wonder why the girl did not simply use her two feet to go exploring about, one must remember that Shintar-Rock is an island drenched with water, and so the most proficient way to travel about is by boat.)

But alas: "Aha," celebrated Elizabeth, when she found a much smaller boat resting by a tree, which was very pretty looking, being completely made of wetted paper pulp and nutshells, mostly that of walnut and almond sort, and a diamond shaped sponge sail.

As soon as the girl placed her feet inside the hull, the boat took off, for the eels had decided to go upstream and the nooses once again played their part.

Elizabeth enjoyed looking at the boat. It had piano key like oars, made of something white and smooth and smelly, with many dancing figures carved within. She felt so inspired by their movements that she too danced about in the boat. Yet, as she twirled about with sudden lurching movements, she smelt something awful: on a patch of sand around a great number of scattered dry grapes, laid two blubbery off-white bodies, dressed in stone boots, trousers, and an egg shaped hat. The girl stared, covered her nose, then her eyes, then her nose again; luckily, the boat did not stop and soon placed the bodies in an away place.

The island itself had many interesting qualities. Though the stream brandished against the boat in little spits of waves, and though the boat fought against the logic of gravity (what goes up must immediately come down without hesitation) it continued to make its way upwards, towards a higher place amongst the mountains.

In any event, Elizabeth placed such illogical superstitions out of her mind and paid particular attention to the flaming trees she passed by every so often.

"How delicious they smell," cried out the salivating girl. "My goodness, is that gruel I see in the trees?"

She was quite hungry, having already digested and disposed of the gruel earlier partaken in; Elizabeth needed new nourishment. However, though tempting, every gruel-tree passed by was covered in scorching flames.

So on she went, up the stream, climbing the mountains, higher and higher.

"Oh my," screeched the girl, for at last a tree vacant of flames had made its way before her.

But how awful it was, for the boat's captains had no intentions of slowing down; the eels had their own journey to fulfill, and the sails and oars looked useless.

Desperate for a mouthful of wonderful gruel, Elizabeth took hold of a few matches and her bucket, for that was all she had time to grab, and leapt into the air, passing the running waters below, and then safely found herself upon dry land next to the inviting gruel-tree.

By this time, the girl's hopes were quite elevated, proven by the drips that began to escape her lips. How grand the gruel-tree seemed to be, filled with balls of utter delight. There were sweet cinnamon gruel-balls and buttery molasses gruel-balls and thick yolky-cheddar gruel-balls and spicy lemon gruel-balls and tart gruel-balls and sour gruel-balls, and more and more kinds of gruel-balls of every sort. She could smell all of their deliciousness's separately and all at once.

But soon a stench overcame the delightful environment, picking at Elizabeth's nose with utter vexation: six blubbery bodies laid on the ground next to the gruel-tree, jiggling in the wind like a colony of blubbery gelatin cakes, exactly like the two she had seen before.

"What was the use of all those nooses then," shouted the girl, annoyed and moderately desensitized by her prior encounter.

In consequence, she quickly turned from the still bodies, tiptoed closer to the gruel-tree, climbed it, picked the ripest gruel balls she could find, taking varieties into account, filled her pale to the uttermost it could possibly withstand, climbed down the gruel-tree, tiptoed in an away direction, and then ran.

Part VII

A QUESTIONABLE CAVE

Elizabeth ran and ran and ran, forgoing comfort of her shins, ankles, and toes, for long and well fed grass placed their blades all around her youthful flesh, seemingly trying to slow her pace; yet, she pressed forth with difficulty, even without much land to run upon, until she eventually stopped at the perceiving of a sound.

"Do not go in there," was the comprehensible warning.

"Is that you?" questioned the girl with a great degree of optimism. "Oh please, it has been so long. Please be you."

And indeed it was.

There the woman with the hoarse voice lay, speaking from a now jumbled mixture in the pale of gruel, which Elizabeth had heroically kept by her side.

"You must listen to me," advised the hoarse-voiced-woman. "There is a dwelling that lies to your left, at an approximate fifteen paces north and twenty-three east; it is a terrible place. You must not go in there, for dreadful things await you if you do. This island is not safe any longer. Quickly, get away!"

Yet, as Elizabeth half listened to the lecture, a terrible concoction of storms developed and blurred out much of what the hoarse voiced woman had warned. In a fraction of a moment, there were rain-storms, and snow-storms, wind-storms, and cloud-storms, earth-storms, and dust-storms, then even molten-storms and amber-storms. The girl felt a surge of emotions and sensations surge throughout her body at the sight, smell, sound, savour, and stroke! stroke! stroke! of it all. It was not at all like the invigorating rain she had experienced earlier. So she quickly ran, losing her bucket along the way, for globs of scotching wet dirt stung her from all directions, banishing the bucket from her side.

To her ill-luck, Elizabeth quickly found shelter at a place that laid fifteen paces north and twenty-three east, which she thought the hoarse voiced woman had instructed her to go to. It was a cave, a dark cave, which is quite a common characteristic, as all such places are famously known to be. Wanting to get rid of the obscurity, the girl took out from her pocket several matches, which were still dry enough to light, lit them, then threw them about to see if anything dry would catch.

"Say tr'n umain," whispered an unseen voice.

"Wee wee wee," was the chorale response.

There seemed to be a choir at hand, and they spoke an inquisitive dialect.

"Please," began Elizabeth, hoping the voices would understand her, "the storm is terrible outside. Can I stay with you for awhile?"

Since a melodic hymn was the only response, the girl left her ears open, placed herself on a rock next to the entrance of the cave, and watched the multitude of storms grapple one another with ferocious weapons, some of heat and others of cold, some of gales and others of zephyrs, and many other things, and all was accompanied by the echoes within the cave and the flashings of light and darkness throughout.

As the girl watched the sky amuse itself with each of the primary colours of the spectrum, and all the mixes in between, especially green, for that is an exceptionally predacious colour, she closed her eyes and enjoyed herself, slumbering into banal dreams of smiles and content.

Part VIII

A DELIGHTFUL DINNER

When Elizabeth awoke, she found herself surrounded by a horde of hermits, each vainly parading drenched robes filled with ruminants of gruel from the gruel-trees, each insatiable degenerate periodically licking themselves, making sure no more gruel laid untouched upon their habits. Though the girl was unsure what the creatures were, she recognized their eyes and intensions; they were like that of her father, the rapacious sort.

Outnumbered, and without hesitation, Elizabeth was bounded and placed within an amber crested cedar barrel filled with Farisian grape water, freshly drenched and dried apricots and Ezilian tomatoes, tickled rosemary, pedantic lavender, darkened fennel, and freshly cut peaches and plums, without the seeds of coarse, and with an addition of Illian pepper to elevate the spiciness; then, when her skin began to wrinkle, perfectly pruned to a ripe consistency, she was transferred to another barrel, this one filled with a delicate jungled honey broth and also a mulled wine, the Clerman and not cheap Hench or Tinglish sort. Then, like a morsel of Cornored veal, the girl was well tended to, that is to say, neglected and constricted to a solitary space, unable to move, only allowed to eat gruel and to take a breath or two or so, now and again, all for maximization of fattening, and thus flavouring. Once plump and well marinated, she was then placed into a heated cauldron filled with a mixture of the marinades and a bouquet garni, of the Hench, then sweetened with more local and delicately collected honey and of that fabled Sadian syrup from the rurals of Tabec, salted with coarse Faysian salt, and finally dribbled with the oil of olives, only the best of the region, of the Kingdom of Qoroccod of coarse.

It was not long before the many flavours mingled and matched, and the hermits were utterly overjoyed at the outcome. Elizabeth was perhaps the most, no, she was the finest urchin they had ever made themselves across, and they were indeed pleased she had made herself onto their table.

After preaching of their humbleness, the hermits rejoiced as they partook in the meal provided by the grace of their maker.

Cutty! Cutty! Cutty!

Sapid bite after bite, they enjoyed themselves to the utter most extent, followed by a raclette, then an ejaculation of merriment and gratefulness:

As we sit in silence, in this lighted room,
Let us partake in our unbridled gloom.

Oh how we all suffer,
But we do it to please,
Now here come the waves
Of our ecstasies.

So here we stay,
And here we lay,
Flesh to flesh,
Quaesïtus est.

look on the next page

The Second Story of This Book About a Child Who Dies

THE STORY OF LIMBO

A Boy, His Journey,

And

What He Met There

Part I

A PLACE IN A HOUSE

Somewhere near somewhere, there was an intricately fabricated house made of exactly five pieces of wood: four were used for the making of its sharp looking walls, which were precisely angled so as not to fall over onto its inhabitants, and the last morceau de bois, as the French say, was for the roof, which was the most cumbersome of the lot, being ill shaped, looking as if it had the stubborn temperament of wanting to squash everything underneath of it. Indeed the house had its good days and its bad days, though never two of the same in a row: sometimes, when the winds became especially excited, the walls acted like sails, catching the testy breeze from this way and that, as if planning to boat its inner vassals unto another place, where brandy flows like hilltops streams and dreams are as sweet as faerie tea; though, it never got to that other side the fictitious brink. On other days, with the same wind, the walls simply played ignorance.

Now onto the inside: Within this simple construction, potato skins were both the somewhat daily delicacy and the staple, which were enjoyed on Tuesdays, Thursdays, and Saturdays, for everyday would be much too royal or rapacious. For the other food source, cabbages, they were gifts to be had only on birthdays. 'Better than the Queen deserves,' the mother of the place would say, whenever finding herself boiling birthday stews, attempting to bring cheery eyes and cherry cheeks to the shivering bones throughout the house. This tenacious figure desperately tried to keep her children's organs going, all eleven of them, at the moment, children that is; though she knew very well that her desires were of the failing sort, for it seemed so often that as one was coming into the world another was waving its hands goodbye.

But let us not get caught up on and in this house, for the day that this story begins was a wicked day for that mother; her son, one of her favourites, Charles IV, whom I will simply refer to as Geoffrey, for my own sake, had enjoyed a several cabbage birthday, a third for each year of his life, and then died.

Yes, he was dead.

Part II

AN IVORY DOOR

Geoffrey had not been a special boy in any particular fashion; he did not have any talents or gifts that he or anybody else knew of. Though he possessed the ability to sing word for word, "God save the King," yes, long live our noble King and all that rubbish, he found it of little value, for he died anyways. Withal, the boy had a strong countenance and heart of approbation for tru'justice, that is, a head for a head, though usually more. Oh yes, he also knew that two potatoes added with another potato meant less potato for him, because any potato that he did not firmly posses was taken away in a whim.

In any event, on this day, after falling asleep next to a carpet of cooling bodies of brothers, sisters, cousins, and so forth, Geoffrey thought it particularly strange that the slap his hand had sent onward towards the sounds of a snoring behemoth, one that deserved to be silenced immediately, for sleep was the boy's only place of solace, was met with a Tok! on a white ivory door.

Startled that he was no longer in a room full of stilling frames, and instead surrounded by another drab, but empty, vastness of darkness, Geoffrey placed himself onto his feet, and then took out a small box of matches he kept safe in his pocket for special occasions of burning things.

There were eight matches.

He lit three.

"By golly!" exclaimed the boy, for before him stood the loveliest door he had ever seen.

Excited by the revelation of his wide-eye peeping, Geoffrey took out a penknife from the same pocket that had produced his earlier treasures and began to carve his name into the pleasant looking tusk. And with the first Scrape! there came a low sounding pound of a musically challenged piano key, undoubtedly an A flat, which was quickly followed by the feeling of a falling jab onto his shoulder.

Now, since the boy was appropriately accustomed to showing off his professed toughness, much like a turtle with a soft shell, he simply ignored the affliction, saying, 'That was nothin,' to himself.

So he continued on with his work.

Yet, with every mark our gracious hero made upon that ivory door, that low A flat noise sounded, and again there was that pain on his person.

"Ts'all nothin I tell you," assured Geoffrey with a continued firmness, as his metal weapon went on tickling with an even greater determination and prowess.

And to a similar degree, so did the three matches that had been forced to life moments ago, if you remember, for they continued to burn bright, consuming their soon to be corpses, until the feverish tribe made themselves known to Geoffrey's waiting fingers.

He dropped all three of them.

They fell toward the ground, though never hitting the one the boy was on.

Even greater fires came to be.

When the boy looked down, wanting to behold what had caught, hoping it was something big and dry, all he could see was a cloud-eyed view of gothically painted pastures whose artist seemed to have had very few available colours for the making, predominantly silver and grey, as well as black and white shades. They were all filled with swaying, dead vegetation and shadowless figures roaming about.

Geoffrey watched, gleefully I might add, as three individual fires burned down below, each concocted by his ostracized matches. Then, one by one, vacant trees, the size of curious elephants, ones too big to stutter, but too small to sneeze, surrounded the burning warmth, only to turn themselves into what they thought would be content ash; yet, the trees hastily grew back into their former selves, much like grass tiptoeing off the edge of a precipice, knowing where oneself should be. Incidentally, no longer was there a flame to attempt distinguishment, only a continued desperation of a bleak sublimating situation.

And then all became dark, again.

Part III

A TREAT OF PIGS FEET

So Geoffrey continued on with his tearing, even though there was no light to support his cause. How the rapacious metal sounded, unsure of where it or its master was, or how they happened to get there: feelings of complexity filled the air. And as the boy did his biddings, so did that one tuned melody, like a symphony of ten, no twelve, pianists, each playing together, as if such a thing was possible, but only having the courage to push down upon that single note: A flat, A flat, A flat; and the pain that fell, ever so unapologetically, began to become unbearable.

Oh what a barbarous situation it was, but Geoffrey persisted, attacking with all his might.

Attack! Attack! Attack!

And then he fell, slipping through the floor.

Down! Down! Down! he went.

The boy was like a falling doorbell: once it sounds, there is never another omen like it, no matter how hard one tries.

Then down some more he went, until he met with the field of grey.

Quite naturally, the ground was a great deal harder than Geoffrey, and considerably sterner to stay in its place, so the boy was displaced when he landed upon it; nevertheless, bones quickly mended themselves back together, slipping here and contorting about to there, into practical positions.

A fine comparison of this situation can be made, and so I will now take the time to do so: It was like that of a recently dishevelled dish of cranberry pie. Though parted for an extended moment by those wretched detaching daggers, the ones who have cast aside the employment of the little dangling fingers and all the spices they bring, and the rest of the sensual limbs who may no longer squish and feel the repast for their bearer's vehement delight, the cranberry globs and buttery crust acquaintances eventually met together again to say their greetings, compressing themselves in embraces, down in the fat man's gut.

Thus, the boy was soon able to put himself back up again, one foot, two feet, very good, so to properly look around. But all was dark; neither hands nor anything else could be seen. There had indeed been no benefit to standing.

A wasted effort.

Eventually, there came a swaying light in the distance, which was cumbersomely paired with something making its way towards our hero; the path it followed was bristled with old corks and pigs feet, all finely edged with elongated swaying grey greensward. How the brightness moved in a hypnotizing fashion, devouringly so.

"Have you anything to eat upon you boy?" were the first words to come out of a plump looking connoisseur of the finest of wines and lards of the swine.

The boy laughed hearteningly, thinking he had been the butt of some well-placed witticism.

"Come now," beckoned the fat man. "Give it here. Don't tell me you're of the temperance sort."

"I ain't givin ya nuthin, I tell ya," assured Geoffrey, thinking the hog was after whatever he had in his pockets; those were his. "Coma foot closah, an yu'll be moppin up ya own gar."

But the gluttonous mind was hungry, and anything moving would do. So the gross gathered up a handful of partaken feet and chucked them forward, forward with faith comparable to that of the shepherd who brought down the deserving ogre to become king of the wandering people; he too prayed to bring down what stood before him and have a line of blood continue forth.

Yet, as Geoffrey was used to having things thrown at him, he had come to possess the cunning ability to elude flying materials; so he was only kicked, or struck, whichever is situationally correct, for I am not sure a dismembered foot counts as a kick, but if it does, so be it, a few times.

And, with much determination, the boy managed to make his way round the grub throwing siege weapon, climbed up the backside of that jiggling tower, took liberty with the voracious's head, and down he went with a quacking force.

The man and mind was dead.

Part IV

BAITING BEARS AND LIZARD TALES

Out of breathe, and quite proud of his doing, Geoffrey took a moment bended, but his activity was directly interrupted.

"Sirrah! I should have been here first," spoke a figure; he was covered in the finest of purple silks and an elaborately adorned white hat as great as the godly king's, I mean, the Servant of servants', silly me, what a mistake? "I am so much better than this and that and this and that, and also that. For heaven's sake boy, where are your manners? Pitiful indeed."

Though only half-interested in an effort to see who was speaking and so stand, the boy was inhibited to fully do so by the aid of a bumptious whip of two tails with tales: one being of a lizard that had not eaten nearly enough to soften itself up, and the other was of a rabbit, one known throughout for being soft, fluffy, and comforting to the touch; Geoffrey was greeted by the prior. So onto his back he found himself, looking up at the swot with contempt.

Indeed it was a man standing before the boy, one like a frog or rat, both being good enough for skinning but nothing else.

"What do you think you are doing?" the vain demanded. "Get back upon your knees, as you should be."

Then another fellow suddenly appeared from somewhere close and interjected, "Don't go trublin t'much. Y'aren't gonna get any outta'at."

"Mumble mumble," was the reply. "Get on! Away! Nothing but a pile of useless scraps."

"Too far," replied the sluggard, which I will now describe in some detail:

The other was a man as well; he was of the slow moving and famished sort. The thing deemed that eating took too much effort, as well as much too much to move other parts, so it was neither of the fat nor fit nor feathery nor frail type. Also, he stunk, and unintentionally dragged a dishevelled non-ticking clock covered in mud behind him; it had somehow gotten caught on his person at one time or another.

The conceited wearer of the fine clothing, perfumes, rhetoric, intellect, et cetera, et cetera, laughed at the sloth and decided to whip him with the lizard tail. For the other, there was not even the sounding of a simple 'Ouch!;' that would have indeed been too great of an effort. So on and on the hitting went, with noises ranging from 'Haha!' to 'Hihi!' but no 'Awa!' or 'Awi!'

The boy, still on the ground, found himself enjoying the two men's dealings to such a degree that elated shivers crawled around his body; it was a good show, like bear baiting or a slip slap at the gallows, without any of that nonsense from niggardly plastering saints.

As the thwack! thwacks continued, Geoffrey was graced with the tale of the lizard: each tryst acted as dictation for its story. And so the boy watched and listened with anticipation, wondering how both would end. For the lizard's tale, it had something to do with a cart filled with an assortment of carrots, blue, green, yellow, crooked, straight, ripe, rancid, but not one good for soup. For the lizard's tail, the beating was quite dexterous.

"Fall down you dull thing," demanded the haughty, for the other was too lazy to make his way onto the ground.

Frustration brought the tail and tale to an end; simple whips would not do. It was time for a graceful attempt at dismemberment. A leg was on the menu.

And so, taking out a golden axe from one of the many compartments within his silk dress, one adorned with marvellous gems of coarse, most likely derived somewhere supposedly grand, the proud man set to work on the other's leg, cutting, cutting, cutting, all around the bone, and then cracked! it off with his bare hands, for he was, as he believed, the only one able to do such fine work.

"Alas!" was the two legged's ejaculation, as the loafer wobbled in his stance and then finally fell. "Now boy—" yet the speech stopped: the speaker was annoyed.

There was a ticking.

"By the Rood! What a ghastly noise," proclaimed He, irritated that the attention had shifted onto something other than Himself.

The lazy so happened to have done much more than ever wanted; he had fallen onto his dirty clock and got it moving.

"Turn him over boy," ordered the egotistic.

"I ain't turnin nu'in ova," rebuked our hero, standing erect, arms crossed: the stance of a champion!

"Sirah! How dare you."

And then Geoffrey was met with the rabbit.

It tickled.

The boy hated being tickled, it was worse than being buried under three feet of dirt, half the way to six; so he turned the reposing man over in order to put a stop to the awful happening. The clock was stuck deep in gut, ticking, ticking; an appropriate redness and pinkness was all about.

"Stop that noise," ordered the haughty.

Geoffrey, worried about having to endure any more of that barbarousness, either within the soon present or at a time that was further away, brought forth a bound of courage, savagely ripped out the clock from the fallen, had an idea, stuck the weapon through the many silk layers of the other, pushed away as hard as he could, and then found a similar softness as the clocks former residence.

"By the hands…of…" struggled the red coloured falling man.

Then there were two upon the ground, sharing their warmnesses of within, which slowly cooled as they mingled; Geoffrey made sure of that. Both eventually became still.

The men and minds were dead.

Part V

It can be deduced that the boy was having quite a pleasant time, more so than, perhaps, ever before. Never had he been so entertained for not even the price of a penny, and that is saying a fair amount, being that he remembered every chance he had ever gotten when excess of coin, beyond that of the need for potato skins, had made its way into his pockets, one way or another. For example, one of the last moments he thought himself amused, for the cost of only three farthings, a bargain, was when he managed to procure a plagued bird for a cock-shying session: all the little one's praised the boy, shooting their sticks with grimaces and gigglings. Oh how exciting and riveting he had thought it all to be. Yet, this time, it cost him nothing, money wise.

So there Geoffrey sat with a smile upon his face; his cheeks dimpling, lips stretching, tongue inside swishing about like the scut of a hare, or an unfortunate chirping cat.

Then he grew bored.

So, to put an end to the travesty, the boy, for the first time since all the eventful happenings, began to wonder where he was; he looked about, though not missing home, questioning where he had woken up in, as well as the appearances of the ghastly men who kept making their way into his direction, and some other seemingly unimportant things.

However, as most of his life's expenditures began with failure, so did this one: all was dark; the light from the fat man had gone out from the ruckus and splatterings. Yet, as he was a clever boy, the matches in his pocket were remembered.

He lit three. Two were left.

Part VI

IN A LIGHT

Brilliantness, like the whispers of a torch's head to a bounding of broken glass, came to be, swaying, uncomfortably visible. And how the mind of a child plays, so did the little bursts of light, skittering about, all birthed by the three matches, ceasing the canvas's smattering colours and shades, as if with bursts of dust clawed from the Diamond's rainbow; no longer were the surroundings of faint shadows on a wall.

Geoffrey thought it, nice.

And though he did try to hold the burning faggots as long as he could, they eventually caused their dispatch, fell, first onto the immaculately adorned white hat of the fresh carcass, catching it alight, then into a puddle of redness they went, distinguishing themselves, extinguishing themselves, purposefully. And then the new blaze began a light of its own, taking away the brilliant newborn, the other, suckling away the colours like a puddle of mud nursing its tender babe, inward cheeks, outward teats; away the splendidness went, until darkness, once again, overcrowded, all but for a dull glow and a straight stream that came from the flaming white hat.

Now, being that Geoffrey was the sort who liked fire, an urge tapped at his fingers, sending the tentacles upon the pretty before him; though this time there came quite a different feeling than the usual. They, his feeling digests and the rest of his person that is, did not burn.

"By golly," the boy exclaimed, though inwardly somewhat disappointed.

So onto his head the treasure went, assisting like a watch tower for wherever he looked.

On his right laid the path of pig and cork; on his left stood one decorated with half empty bottles of spiced rum.

"A fine time, I tell ya," assured Geoffrey to himself, venting the sweet liquor into his nostrils.

The boy did not bother looking in the other directions; a self-libation was to be had.

Part VII

BURNING! BURNING! THAT MAKES THREE

So off to the rum garden Geoffrey went, grooming his puckering lips with swooshes from the nightingale between his teeth, enthusiastically in expectation to soon be singing to the King, as is the only spirit one can; and after grasping the cool bottle, raising it up from its fallen state, twisting the harbinger's spout sideways, making sure that his face funnel was as wide as could be, and while his stomach yearned for the bottle's innards, for delicate spices and warmness, a wild looking beast fellow intercepted the boy and his wanting, bringing them both to the ground. The wrath bashed him with closed hands, the wroth of a vicar preaching possession of the Spirit itself, while slews of foam sludged down from the edges of the man's mouth as well, spilling onto Geoffrey's jerking head, like the droppings of a scavenging vulture, marinating its prey with excess.

But being our hero had often found himself in such situations, after a few cowardly blows from the dastard, up flew the boy, twisting his body to freedom; and then he broke a bottle onto the savage's head.

The man laid bleeding, but not completely beaten.

The hat laid alone, but not far, projecting its light onto the scene.

"I'll ave at you boy," proclaimed the hate. "Don't think you'll be gettin away so easy."

In response to the threat, Geoffrey met the man with another bottle, soaking him with more of the toothsome rum, which in turn brought quietness from the ill-anger for the moment being.

And similarly to the last encounter of men, the sin was not alone, for within a moment another came, this one singing of spring and birds and things.

"Thank goodness I have found you," began the libertine. "Oh at last! At the very moment I set my eyes upon your delicate features, how my heart began to beat, like a fox playing upon a rabbit hole, or a dove pecking into a worm pole. Come here boy. Oh you. Wait a moment. No. Drink first. Drink until your heart is content. Fill your blessed cheeks. Fill your blessed heat until it peaks, until the air it sleeps narrowly with sweets."

And indeed the boy was thirsty, for after such recent undertakings would not anyone be?

So Geoffrey indulged himself, enjoying the sting upon his lonely throat, the warmth dripping by his lungs, finding its ways all through his arms, fingers, from head to down below; all the while, the rake sang a wanton song of woe:

"It hurts! It hurts! How the pain it hurts and bursts; within my purse is worse. A curse! You have bewitched me! But you are my salvation. You, the temptation, an incantation of my desires and fires. Please, set me free. Please bring me glee. On hands and knees I bow, your slave, as you are my cave, my shelter, my aid. It is your duty, for your beauty is beyond compare, like that of falling rain, it stains me bare. Oh pain! Oh pain! Oh pain!"

When the man finished his customary lament, the boy voiced, "Whadya goin on about?"

And the lust's reply, "He speaks! He speaks! And with such a pre-bloom." Geoffrey did his own doing as the licentious went on, "If there was but more of time in itself, I would fall onto your sword a thousand deaths a thousand times over. To fill you with even a single drop from my eye, it would bring me to my knees, over and over again. Oh if—"

Luckily for the boy, not having much in his stomach, he quickly fell to the heaviness of his libation; and to his benefit, being an ill tempered sort of enthusiast, he shot his fists forth, straight at the lecher, who was still going on; yet, our hero tripped, falling, pushing his target over, who landed right onto the hat and burned and burned until only the hat remained.

How the fire was delightful.

But it did not stop there.

As rum laid everywhere from the recently dismembered bottles, much about caught fire, including the other man who did not seem to mind in the least; he seemed to enjoy the raging flames and the bursting bottles all around, for he continued to lie still, presumably enjoying himself as much Geoffrey.

That rare smile once again projected itself like a Midsummer's night.

And to make three, an other of envy ran onto the pile of flames and burned away as well.

The men and minds were dead.

Part VIII

CLINKER TINKER

The spectacle now over, the boy picked up the fallen hat with a leisurely temperament, placed it back onto himself, pressed forward through the field of broken bottles, and then beyond that place of choleric temperaments, until he found himself some place else.

The novel surroundings were quite. The air still. It reminded Geoffrey of peaceful nights, those spent curiously counting stars, listening to nothing but an overcrowded void: the humming of his own throat and the desperate moans around him. Yet, though the boy directed his eyeballs towards what he thought to be the heavens, hoping to meet with the watching Angels of a sleeping sun, there were none: only a stretched stream of light and a surrounding blackness.

"Ts'all poesies" cursed the boy, frustrated by the bootylessness of his efforts.

Now there was most certainly nothing in the least interesting to look at or do. The place seemed absolutely, positively boring. So down laid Geoffrey, shutting his peepers, attempting sleep.

Moments past. Then more. But nothing came.

Another wasted effort.

The very idea of sleep mocked him. Nevertheless, realistically, there was no way of escaping from the present consciousness; dreams were no longer at an appropriated disposal, or should we call them nightmares, as many dreams are.

Then suddenly, as if to teasingly shatter the dullness made from its prolonged absence, a residue of that lame toned A flat sound sounded. The pitch was as it had been when next to the ivory door of long ago, the place where the boy had etched his name away, so devoutly, or courtly a dolt might say.

Cutty. Cutty. Cutty.

A short Interlude:

Now, a moment is to be taken,
After ceasing continuation,
For as is know of contemplation,
The sort of youthly impregnation,
All much too fleeting when awaken.

Thus, prepare your holly wits my miss,
For a fancy gist will be in this,
Not the nasty sort that blinds the wits,
But those of salted gore-fowls that kiss.

And so a moment taken, let us proceed:

Though the following previously occurring event may have passed much too quickly for the extended observation of a glance, it nevertheless took place during Geoffrey's fruitless attempts at sleep: A gargantuan flying elk, as if appearing out of an empty wooden box from the bottom of a well, had swooped down and swallowed the boy whole. This fine creature, naturally adorned with crystal skin and the sweetest of venison, was forever followed by a pack of dangling rabid wolves, each attached to the beast by silver collars and chains fashioned from lead; the danglers were not of the flying type nor were they as appealing to the eyes and tongue as the prior.

In any event, the title of the fair swallower is as follows: Felk. And for the benefit of additional information, let it be known that much folklore surrounds the meetings and histories of Felk and its kind, most notably the story of Felk and the Moon, a most wondrous tale if you ask me.

And for the fate of our hero, the reason he had heard a piece of that A flat sound was because, after being forcibly devoured so suddenly so, the creature had spit him out, due to gastric informalities, and as God's will, so found himself back in the room in front of the ivory door; though, as for the fate of the helpful hat, it had found itself placed further down the swallowing tube, so did not follow suit in the regurgitation.

Being strong willed, Geoffrey picked himself up immediately after the happening, licked his palms, heard chinking noises, pressed his hands into his pocket, took out the remaining matches within, and brought them to life.

He lit two. None were left.

"Oh, I see!" rejoiced a newly exposed chosen man, surrounded and covered in coin.

Yes a man.

The boy's eyes shimmered at the circles of gold and silver, each of them breathing out a hollow glow upon their present owner. And as Geoffrey stared, he unfortunately realized that his burning things were almost finished with their self-consuming ritual, so he removed what little clothes laid upon his body and put them to better use, so the roommates thought.

"Stay away boy," attacked the avarice acquaintance. "This is mine, not yours. Turn your head away and look somewhere else."

But Geoffrey monastically assured himself with a mantric devotion that he could not help himself to look away; he did this until he eventually successfully convinced himself on the matter.

He wanted the coins. He wanted them all.

"Gimmim now!" demanded our hero.

But the rapacity would not divorce with a single token; it was not law. Even though they fertilized themselves, unnaturally, hatching more gold and more silver, beyond usefulness, not one would be spared.

The boy imagined the wolfish tippling such coin could bring to himself, feeling conceited that he would never need to exert another moment of effort, except for when brought to a fury by those who would not alleviate future goatish desires. How he wanted what the other had. How he required all of it.

Looking around to find something of aid, Geoffrey discovered, lying next to the ivory door, his old friend: the pen knife; it had remained in the room during his absence. This time however, instead of dedicating himself to the sculpting of his name, the boy took an advantage, making it so that the greed could no longer voice any opposition: a tickle to the chest and a few dabs to the neck took place. Yet, as Geoffrey did so, that A flat and that jab upon his shoulder made themselves freshly known in unison, again and again.

A flat! A flat! A flat!

And then down! And down! The boy went.

Geoffrey fell through the floor of the room back into the field of greyness, so did his enkindled clothes, and found himself surrounded by deadpan trees, attempting to make use of the fallen flames. Our hero had a sensibility to do the same, and so ran with the others towards and into the light, not to tease the burning, but to put himself out. Yet, after catching and not turning into content ash, all were trees again.

So was Geoffrey.

The fire went out.

The boy was in the Story of Limbo.

look on the next page, again

The Third Story of This Book About a Child Who Dies

A Place Somewhere Over-Ground Or The Place of Over-Ground

Annabella's Journey...
In a Place Most Likely too Difficult for the Dull
Minded to Comprehend,
Or the Malcontent,
Or Dim Witted,
But I Digress

An Author's And reader's Acquaintance In Order To Better Understand The Following Story Involving The Girl Named Annabella

Somewhere, there was a girl.

Yet, before going on any further and extrapolating upon an unexpected following, an account that contains that of the most evocative and sensational events, situations that will surely leave the reader wondering why? and how? and this? and that cannot be true! (but I assure you it is, definitely so) it must be noted that Annabella, the girl of this tale, was a crafty youngling of the most peculiar sort, per say, if said can be so: For some unexplainable reason, this exceptional being had the particular capability of manipulating certain situations around her so as to procure her every fancy, even to that of the most minute and trivial of happenings, if she ever so wanted.

"How could such a thing be?" I am guessing is your inquisitive reaction to the later, my dear reader. Well, it was as so, just so. You can either ignore this fact, or even deny it, if that is what meets your fancy, but in the end, truth be told, what has been said is true, undeniably so, and your opinion or conviction is quite worthless on the matter. So please, let our argument not digress us any further from this narrow path of concentration, one that we have both agreed to travel upon during a most questionable portion of our lives.

Now I'll continue on and let this story grow.

Some Growing

Strangely, if I may use the word attentively, even though Annabella could in essence posses everything and anything her heart could ever desire, from that of mountain trees, to that of the very wind and light that trickles and gushes between the leaves of its offspring; she was nevertheless an enchanting young girl, not odious to any degree. Particularly, and regrettably, she had an unforgettably thoughtful demeanour; this is to say, she hardly ever used her natural ability to achieve any self-centered advancing advantages; though, like us all, narcissism trickles down into the wanton pond now and again, especially when past pain is to be ritually repeated.

However, before continuing and projecting any heart felt ejaculation onto how quaint such a literary situation should be, I must request a moment of remembrance and contemplation, as time more often than not, I hope, proves to benefit those who identify with the naïve species of the ignoramus: thoughtfulness does not equal a situation's entirety. For, it should be noted, thoughtfulness is only a part of a doing, the other being that of the desired treatment of those affected.

As an author, and self-esteemed philosopher, I have often contemplated on the matter, creating vast consolations of my own well-worn philosophies regarding the dialectic intricacies of the matter, manipulation. But lo and behold, the debate continues on without a decidable ending, one to which I try and hold onto, so to excuse the pain I have caused.

But to bring short this philosophical and philanthropic rant, I hope it has not already turned you off onto other things, such as the glossing of words of a disparaging sort throughout and upon the sides of these very words in the margins of these very pages.

While the girl tried to act for the benefit of others, she, for the most part, happened to act in a way that gave others what they did not want. Though caring, Annabella was at a loss when trying to understand the desires of others: though she was a character of sensibility, one able to gasp and then sigh at the sight of a child who has only one glove; or tear up and then faint at the sight of a solitary bird, harrowingly ostracized by some unnamed brute, now to forever be idolicized inside of its cage; or even pull out her lovingly locks and beat her chest blue at the sight of a withered beggar asking for spare pennies; she was not skilled at sympathy. Though she attempted whole-heartedly to make others happy, delighted, content, satisfied, etcetera, she unceasingly brought on the very opposite of the others' desires.

Now that this introduction is over, let us get on with the emotionally plump story of Annabella.

But First A Wee Bit More

Annabella, the noble hearted one, was born someplace underground. She had lived in the particular predicament for a total of, well, let us say, several years now. How often she had thought of what it would be like to burrow deep up to the dirt that lay above her head, pressing on until she found something fanciful and wonder filled.

And so often she did try.

And every time she did fail, oddly enough.

You see, the girl had heard various oral tragedies of the 'Up-lings' (that is, the name given to those who live above; for those who live bellow, I suppose you may call them the 'Down-lings,' though such a name seems quite ridiculous, but I deviate). Because of this, her mind had become essentially and unequivocally use to racing within itself upon the various possibilities of what could and perhaps did exist in the places placed in that up direction. The accounts made her frantic with such curiosity and desperation that she began to live in the fantastic world within her head in bed, creating entirely new situations in which she effected in some form or fashion.

Part I

AND NOW TO THE BEGINNINGS OF THE HAPPENINGS
THAT HAPPENED INTO THE CHARATER OF THIS STORY:
ANNABELLA

On a mid-spring's night's eve, when lovers begin to seek themselves into supposedly dissembling and cloaking bushes and woodlands, where ready rebels go to stain the white robe among the forbidden grassy maidenhair greens, Annabella sat alone within a room, one she had slept within for the majority of her existence, trying to decide what thoughts she wished to bring with her to the shadows and phantoms of the dream land.

She stared into hollowness and thought, bemoaning over that of which had so often met with her, that of which she believed, in some way, could never be met with again, or which she hoped perhaps would not.

Harpooning into her mind's looking glass, she decided to grasp at the idea of a long nosed, sordid creature stuck in a tree of ripening fruit.

So off to bed she made herself, quickly clapping her feet towards a place of ruffled sheets made from the purest of golds, which could be said to have been spun so thinly in their making that they could be compared to the likes of birthing clouds, each daintily placed upon a puddle of dew, as delicate and hesitant as could be. And the pillows, the pillows were the likes of a thousand sheep and a thousand swans, the later of which could be said to still be trickling their final songs, ones so affecting that the muses themselves often mused upon them.

And as the girl placed herself upon her hardened knees, ones that had been so often forced to fall upon, for the desire of the good Master, forever and ever, amen, she felt a brave rush of courage towards something that had long been a struggle within herself: Annabella stood up and jumped out a window.

She fell, and fell, and fell.

But instead of falling to a certain death below, where there happened to be a mound of ready spikes, feverish beasts, and reptiles hungry for soft flesh, and depthless waters waiting to constrict and bury any newcomer beneath (oh yes, I so happened to forget, and so left out, the part of the girl being trapped within the middle to top area of an ostentatious tower, which she had been forced to stay within because…well that is quite obvious, no need to patronize) she in actuality fell in the upwards direction instead.

So up and up she went, passing through the ground that had always laid above her head, just as if she had taken a dull knife and forced it through a rotten tomato, or a rancid plum, or someone or something that causes one to be unable to make oneself any further beyond their pain or undeserved predicament.

Cutty! Cutty! Cut! As some might say.

But then Annabella became stuck, six feet, or some many half-cubits, underground. Nevertheless, she was indeed where she was, and so pressed herself upwards, pushing and pulling, feeling closer and closer to the surface's top. And inch-by-inch, she made herself towards the above, never for a moment running out of breath, for if she had, this would have been quite a short story.

Imagine the following: a green pasture, untouched for time, precious, chaste, never having been broken, bled, or littered with pernicious excrement; where fragrant flowers let free their senses and scents without the dangers of having their-selves taken; where grass flows strong and as delicately as the waves upon its river's edge; where the sands of its bays and the moss that tickles upon and against its trees are mounted on one another, only for the purposes of mutuality.

Now, imagine the following: a bleak and empty sublimating situation; where the dirt is as black as coal, not because it is bountiful with nutrients, but because it is gluttonous with devilry; void of light; where the survival of the cruelest dominates.

The later is our current situation, one paraded as the prior.

Part II

HURRAY! AN UP-LING

Out from beneath said black-crusted soil, sprung a collected assortment of insistent and dirt-sodden fingers. Then followed a full hand, an arm, another hand, and another arm.

Though many might have given up and succumbed to the constriction of such an underground encasement, Annabella pressed forth with tenacity, pressing her palms like psalms away from the soil that lays beneath all living feet, and pushed herself upwards and outwards until her soles were able to breath in what they believed to be a place of ecstasy, for the surroundings were new and different, and such things tend to give such ignorant impressions.

The girl took in deep breaths, trying to fill herself with the suspicious air between her teeth; yet, having to get use to its impotent altitude of breathability, she was forced to lay upon her back for several moments, inhaling and exhaling profusely, until finally, able and ready to look at what had become to surround her; she speculated about where she was.

Soon enough Annabella realized that she had become an Up-ling.

A Brief Interjection Made By The Author In Order To Aid the reader In Understanding And Sufficiently Following The Story At Hand

Though it may seem startling, it has already been more than something like a year since the last time we met. Either you are a special sort of slow reader or some inescapable tragedy has torn you from these pages, thus the cause of delay.

Nevertheless, much has happened since our last encounter, though you have no entitlement to know what occurred exactly, only that the situations and happenings involved our hero and some peculiar predicaments.

Thus in any event, Annabella was now a wanderer, one known throughout the famous land and beyond as 'The Harborous Maiden of the Forest,' for as the accompanied maxim went, 'It is better to bury oneself within the bottom of an eternal cave of desolate isolation then meet face to face with The Harborous Maiden of the Forest who will certainly bring about a fate most unexpected,' but I foreshadow.

Part III

WHAT DOES A MAGGOT HAVE TO DO WITH ANYTHING?

On the forecasted day in which we re-join this most humble of stories, Annabella was in the midst of enjoying a scrumptious strawberry in a field filled with the most delicate and difficult to pronounce of fanciest of fruits, peculiar produce that thus satisfies the pallets of even the most picky of tongues, no matter their offset emporium.

And on and on she enjoyed that strawberry (entirely unaware that only three days prior, a buker of a hoary bloke had been picking some of the same delicious fruit as she, in the very same place as she, for the particular purpose of pressing upon a misses that he had placed his eye towards so fervently the day before, but being old and fragile, he had lost one of his fingers while culling away, which inevitably led to a big gush of red, until the whole man fell apart and made a big mess that would have probably taken an entire afternoon to clean up if it had happened indoors) nibbling, swishing, playing with the seeds and fleshy parts from one side of her tongue and cheeks to the other, letting the juices ferment before permitting them to slide down her throat and eventually into her intestines and finally to and beyond her bowls.

But then the girl choked: She had attempted the swallowing of much too big a piece of fruit; and, if the reader has not yet deduced, something that would certainly not surprise me, the main events of this story were about to begin.

In an astute display of hysterics, one that would surly impress the solemn tigress of an opium den, or the feverish still member of a decanted eye, Annabella stumbled several stones throw forward, an eternity it seemed, until she fell onto a log, landing like a rag doll upon her stomach.

But oh, dear reader, what could have happened next? Did our dear girl survive? Did she die? No. Is such a fate to be expected? If so, ask yourself why.

Despicable.

In any event, there so happened to be, before the fall, a maggot busy upon some unidentifiable remnants on said log, an attractive one, maggot that is, with a translucent crumply body and silvery sparkling teeth, and drool, which was silver too.

For character introductory and fleshing out purposes, read the following: Said the maggot sometime before the current event:

Some days past, before the mentioning of journeys,
There happened to be a starveling, a posh boy,
Who thought he to be beyond the need of gurneys,
That is, till he tried to loot the fruit of some goy.

It all began by a bucket of beans, I'm told,
When the child made mockery of the fat cock,
A girl, much too dreadful, and also much too cold
To be of any use for the gentile hock.

Yet, when he saw the lass, the boy forced out his hand,
Reaching for her sack: a harvest, one of fresh fruit.
But the goy closed that door, the most beautiful land,
Where blunted desire captures itself in route.

Thus, the boy fell in place, love sick with desire...
But joy, he was dead, ready to feed my fire.

And through and through said sonnet storyteller made itself within and all over the deceased degenerate, slicing and munching on even the most questionable of parts, on and on, and on and on; for days and days the man-eater did its natural due diligence, hard at work. What a committed creature, dedicating itself, heart and soul, to its task, turning lips into plump decay, nose into slushy flakes, and then some and then some, eventually followed by the eyes, which popped spectacularly after a thorough poking into.

Now, we turn back to Annabella: When the girl had finished falling, she squashed the busy maggot entirely. There was nothing specific left of it, not even if one wanted to scrape up and turn it into an unadulterated rancid mush pod, one day to metamorphosis into the bastardization of an elegant moth, ostensibly to be rejected by a deflective family of pejorative pesticides.

But oh how the beauteousness felt at what she had done: it was to be an awful fate for some.

Annabella would never want such a happening to occur; if only it had been her that she had fallen upon. She could see herself become as flat as a palm branch, laid upon a dirt path for the servant of the poor to trod upon—if only she would be so lucky to be his majesty's used napkin.

And so, being the girl felt awfully responsible, she desired to the uttermost extent that the poor maggot had not suffered its final destination as it had, but instead would undergo some other fate, one completely different from what it had so unfortunately experienced.

This wish left options quite open to interpretation.

And as she desired, so it commenced.

Part IV

SOMETHING OCCURRED

Up and in and out from the ground, the resurrection of
the broken maggot was inaugurated; a renewal of life was
breathed back into its mushy body. Yet, while the thing
began to fidget and spew out commercial sounds of
rejuvenation, like that of Sephardic peacocks in heat, so too
did the sprauncy boy it had gluttonously fed upon: each of
the fresh and fermented in-nards and out-nards collected
themselves, forming one single creature.

To make matters a little clearer for those who are unable,
or should I say incapable (laughter) to keep up with the plot
and subject matter, for reasons I will not explicitly judge as
pathetic, as such things are of a baser delicacy, I will
delicately explain within the following chapter this earnest
occurrence in the uttermost of simplest of summaries.

Part V

A RESURRECTION

i) A vague alternative fate for the maggot was desired.
ii) The maggot was brought back to life.
iii) The boy as well.
iv) The maggot and the boy combined into one thing.

Part VI

THIS IS WHAT HAPPENED NEXT

And forth both things sprouted, turning quite into their ugly former likings, as neither the maggot nor (for the purpose of this story we shall call him...) Peter were attractive looking creations, even though the latter had been moulded from clay/dirt/other in a specific image(s), and the former as the original companion for the latter, eventually to be outdone by the fairer sex (exegesis for yourself).

While Annabella had specifically wished for the maggot's condition, and only the maggot, unaware of its recent meal, the amount of attempted sympathy put forth inevitably led to a generous overflow, spreading like a barrel full of indigent children, so that the boy's involvement un-expectantly became a luxurious, or inconvenient, or perhaps to the reader, a dramatic, consequence: the two were taken from the trash fires as one wedded form, looking like a stunted hoodlum made of translucent midget worms, dripping its squirmy little grubs from the slightest of movements, each sack clear enough to witness the putrid workings, while seemingly blinding enough to put on a delusion of outward courtliness.

The girl made a sound in reaction to the topical appearance, and then clapped her hands, hummed, smiled, circled her eyes twice round, and then twiddled all of her toes again and again, making sure to express her great excitement towards the whole subject and matter at hand.

"Scuse meh mis," sounded the ugly abomination, "but is you lookin fo sum peice? Coughs came paired with vomits of maggots as the thing tried to persuade her with a smile.

Acting as if there was one in its pocket, "Is fo you if you gat any fru ta shayah."

Now, as we know, I hope by now, I truly do, Annabella was of the most considerate of sorts; so, when she heard the voice of the maggot-boy, her heart ba-beated between her unsung breasts in the most rigorous of manners, twisting the strings of the tattered and artistically potent, clenched fates; how she wished and wished that the thing she thought of at the present moment would be the most happiest and pleased of living things that there has or ever could be: She truly wanted the thing to feel individualistic satisfaction.

And so it did.

The maggot-boy became a haughty coxcomb to the extent that it began to jitter like an old burning faggot covered in an assortment of coloured pixy sticks; so naturally, the maggot-boy struck its fingers into its mouth, I know I would, and strategically pulled them out, after momentary sucking, to show fineness; yet, unused to the current state, the thing's dexterous playing led to the ejaculation of a prodigious pile of maggots from it's person, ones that quickly broke from their fleshy selves into a buzzing swarm of fevered flies, all of the wanting temper. And to indulge their palates thoroughly, the nearby trickling dung of a horde of somewhat paired dead birds was now on the menu.

So they made themselves away.

"Oh my," shouted the maggot-boy in an ecstasy of joy. "I do believe dat I'm da luckiest der's ever ben. I fel so happei."

Oh how the girl smiled at the thing's heartfelt utterance. She felt so pleased that he/it had become to be filled with such joy and evocative felicity of the bodily sort.

(ahem) Let me cut in at this specific strategic moment, as the end, brace yourself, is near.

You see, our hero (My, I have only called her that once throughout this entire story, and that was quite a few pages back, all the way in the interjection. Well, I will give her the majestic name once again, with pride and certainty. Our hero, yes, our hero, our hero... our...(cough) our...I believe it has grown out of fashion already. Alas, let us continue to call her something else from now on, perhaps, simply, the girl. Yes, that fits nicely, as well as her name, Annabella) had spotted an ugly thing covered in a hordes of drab, mismatched, and loose cloth: a witch.

Oh how the thing looked on in desperate contempt, for it knew what had spotted s/he.

And as we, the knowledgeable, know nothing good comes from an un-beautiful witch, for the beautiful always share, if even a little, a moment of bliss, but yet we speak of the other, especially the ones that promise all that there is, good, and then secretly the worse, or the heart shape fog of a curse, love; yes, I speak of this curse.

But Annabella, unfortunately, or fortunately, did not.

The End

Now, the girl wondered what the thing could be, you see, Annabella had never seen such a thing as she. So our... the girl... crooked her mind about, waiting... waiting... and waited.

My, she waited even more!

And then some more (as you may expect from my past artistic endeavors).

Though it may seem like a dull undertaking for some, Annabella waited in that very exact place, fixed, still as a broken mill, stagnant, unflinching, to the point of resembling a frozen fish gill, stuck to bake on a rock in the heat of a treacherous pilling afternoon, seemingly, and expectantly, lifeless, until the Georgian, or then Victorian, date of summer, the time when flowers are finished with their spirited loom, dull and no longer rash as in their fullest bloom, but of coarse on their way to a wrinkled doom, and the birds, a time when brashness and being elegantly pruned is no longer within the popular tune, the brightest are done with their wanton and dexterous moons, and the leftovers chitter bitter songs of gloom; yes, this very specific time and date.

And the girl waited and waited, making sure to take the utmost of time to observe all that was around her, making sure she did not misinterpret the thing that she had suddenly discovered.

Yet, so did the witch stay still, and so did the maggot-boy against his will; the two things waited, neither able to move from their place.

They waited.

The later seemed perfectly fine, for when maggots die, as all who have conducted the experiment are aware, others born themselves from the decay, metamorphosing into smaller, refreshed, and rejuvenated larvae.

The state of the witch was of another matter, however. She did not have the same vitals and makings of the maggot-boy, only superficially related; instead, her form was made of the usual, ordinary composition of a corpse, including the such, like lungs, spleen, and green bowls of cream. But, because of the thing's waiting and waiting, she had shriveled up into what could only be described as a dry, hollow looking thingumajig. She was more of the likes of the dust from a posh-man's pocket, filthier than anything living, if ever she was.

To give even more helpful information regarding the specifics of the situation, the only reason the witch had the ability to continue on with her breathing, and thus had not immediately burst into a bank of smouldering flames, or floated to the top of a river in chains, was because, and you might find this highly coincidental, but I assure you it is not, instead it is highly factual, highly indeed, she had just come from a potion symposium held by a somewhat competent alchemist in training. In effect, she had engaged, to put politely, with a few different concoctions of the most variable and miscellaneous of sorts, and one seemed to have worked in her sort of favour on this paulista of many days and nights. Though, she still felt the hunger, the agony of being pressed to a spot with no escape, month after month, day after day, hour after hour, and, well, so on and so forth.

But Annabella was deep in thought and needed most of what surrounded her to stay utterly and absolutely still, in order for correct interpretations to take place.

Time came and then time went, pressing to pass as if cast to silently sing upon the subtle curves of a pubescent's glorifying looking-glass.

Lada, tada, tadi; tomatoes, hibiscus, sardines. (Just imagine the apocryphal ridge and someday it will come to you) oops, forgot the period/full stop, there (.)

Then a realization of a sight came before the girl; she had waited so long to properly deduce her situation that a pack of weasels, or to be more broad, of the meat eating mammals of the mustelidae family, had decided to make a home underneath the thing's (the witch's) assortment of cloths, bones, hair, and whichever homey, useful debris was left after the mentioned passing of time.

Oh how the girl thought the happening to be of the most joyous of occurrences. Her face fingers stretched in a fashion of delight, and her eyes pressed together as if groping a stretchy sausage mid flight.

In a heat of great sorts, she wished the witch to stay waiting as it was, forever to be in that place, for the happiness of those who now habited underneath were so— well, if the protagonist of this story would have ever spoken a word, she would have surely said—wonderful.

And then the girl saw the maggot-boy.

He too was much like the witch, frozen and pressed into place, but he was of another use to the weasels. Instead of an item of shelter, the maggot-boy had become, or to be perfectly, politically correct, formed into, an item of nourishment, something the mammals could nibble, squish, or suck at whenever in need of a bitter reminder, or diversion as the laymen call it, or something to occupy the stagnant and stale state of breathing, of life.

Nevertheless the politics, Annabella found both the happening of the witch and the maggot-boy to be marvelously wonderful events, and quaint, as she wished for the weasels to continue on with their abode and newly acquired life-style, sniffing and digging, sleeping and oblivious to the hardships and dumb of the unforgiving world, one adjacent to the smallest of pious jewels, each and every picketed from the pockets of fools.

And so the time never came when both of said characters took their last breaths and died, for all stayed as they were, perched on continuity and faith to their elongated state of conformity.

Forever.

Here Lies Another Chapter?

Though I Am Not Sure How Well the reader Will Take It, As I Do Realize That I May Have Led There To Be The Expectation Of An Immediate Ending With The Last Chapter Title, But I Assure you That I Will Now Finish The Story Off, For True. However, Yes, There Is A However, While the reader May Be Preparing themselves For An Ending That Will Surely Satisfy their Peculiar, Per Say, And So So Refined Taste, I Do Have To Warn That they Are Most Likely Too Dull To Be Able To Fully Appreciate The Magnificence That Stands Before them.

Nevertheless, Here Follows The Final Chapter Of This Story.

Chapter, The Finale. En Petite.

In actuality, this is a short story after all; I do not feel like writing any more.

THE END

Chapter: Untitled

Section I

A FORSAKEN CONTINUATION

It is quite true that this story was suppose to end as it just did, but after a few weeks of thoughts of thinking and then thinking it over, I thought something was missing, and this is what that something was, or at least close enough:

Not long after Annabella had finished gluttoning upon the sights before her, making a suppositional loyal clan of the stinking, egg sipping, hen clipping, sots, a sort of merriment she had long wished for but had escaped her beneath the sludge of immortal nightmares and dreams, like a vassal of unvoiced choir folk, swaying to the sip of the Father's leaded cup, she became satisfied, and then inevitably jaded, as all ostentatious things eventually do, an inevitable growth to the plain and ordinary from even the most beautiful and pleasurable, and so went on her way into and through a supplanting weed plantation of sorts, wandering through the likes of coffer-webs and nightmare-weeds, each and each made of oozing, prickly honeyed death, and then on and on and into and beyond woodlands of dangling piggish branches of the grimacing sort, hungry to snatch onto, wrap around, rip into, and bubble from within the womb of any formidable flesh within their grasps, pleased to play the game of topsy.

This went on and on, etcetera, etcetera, until a yellowish light in the near distance, one as dull and lacking as the first sun's rise after a lover's funeral, but more or less noticeable than a swine-lantern stuck within a creeping cave on a hallowed night, fading in and out, oh so opportunely, showed itself, and took hold of the girl, metaphorically dear reader.

For what seemed to be a mismatched extended moment, Annabella followed herself towards that bewitching brilliance until she arrived at a half-town, one borrayed (i.e. purposefully covered, but to ill effect) in green painted fox-leathered crates, filled with simple, though a little reddish, ostrich eggs.

I kid you not.

And near to where she stood, huddled around a straight and extravagantly tended field of Napoleon grass, were holistically placed flophouses, all of which independently presented themselves in the most inviting of manners, doors extended and open and all. Each of the jades were skillfully built, erected, promoted as to demonstrate its creator's irrevocable ability to sneeze or squeeze something out of its tender eye, something so complex and simple, as if created from and for the knottiness of life.

Nevertheless, it was the yellowed sight that filled her head-pocket with interest, so much so that Annabella became compelled to take a step towards its place of origin, then another, though of coarse all the while respectfully expressing her expected polite mannerisms of admiration and the awe due towards the other humble surroundings.

She looked up. She looked down.

She looked left. She looked right.

Then she continued to look straight into the light.

Section II

A CLOWN

As if at a competition to snuff out one another for the girl's attention (or a talented writer's excuse at moving on with the story at hand), a most interesting thing produced itself from Annabella's charitable lookings: a (I want to say sordid, but I'm not sure the description fits exactly) creature, much like a open-faced-clown, one who has drunken much too much blueberry juice (yes, that's it!), decorated in the most elegant of tinsels, buttons, and bells, jingled itself out from one of the houses, until it was directly before the girl; it held out a flightless bird egg and a chest-clock, both the size of a very large dried cranberry, so she could see them explicitly.

"If only," suddenly began the creature, oh so elegantly, though in a contorted but somewhat refined tone and dialect, "your heart would churn to a blubbery gloop inside yourself. Does it girl? Does it now?"

Annabella looked on, not with intrigue, but with a caring intention, for the blue-mouthed thing seemed quite stressed and was in much need of something strong.

He then continued, after dismissively chucking the weighty egg yolk into a bush, "You see, I have a clock that has laid around my neck for as long as a heart can remain broken, but the item means so little or ever so much to me when I think beyond the simplicities of where its arms and legs frolic themselves, at any moment, day or night, when I am not or am looking that is. Every other crack in time, you see, I hear a 'tick,' or better yet, a melodic death tone, sounding itself, a clank that can bring the least ancient of sorts to a fit of reminiscent spews of the times passed and had, either of want or regret. But to me, only a worthless sound, you see, one of mockery, a most cruel reminder of depravity, pounds within my ear, like a serpent in need of an ardent repose. There is no one to see the decrying thing go…'tock.'"

Though the girl had no idea what the soppy-clown was going on about, admittedly a little preoccupied by the watching of his oval bracelets and puckish cheeks go round and round their distracting axes, much like cotton balls within a camel's mouth, she nevertheless smiled, as she hoped her agreeing would bring the poor sap some joy in some way or other.

Alas, her doings seemed to prove beneficial to her goal, for the dinging man put on a grimace, calling forth a protrusion of yellowed teeth and frost bitten lips, or half-lips would be more accurate, from that place that for some reason has been chosen as the token stage for happiness. Annabella nodded her head in slow sapient motions, which proved to be even more emotionally affective, as the thing began to fidget. Encouraged, the girl placed an even wider smile upon herself, showing the brilliance of her youthful face bones, that rare virtuous team, and rocked her head more quickly and with much more rigor.

Though the ugly-clown felt some sort of positivity from Annabella's visual display of sensibility, he felt a suspicion that his audience was completely ignorant to his complaint, and she was simply agreeing to appease his inner thirst for understanding and acceptance.

To test out his hypothesis, he recounted the following somewhat related parable:

Section III

THE PARABLE

There was a dwarf who had the desire to swim across the most traitorous of rivers, for on the other side supposedly lived a beautiful mistress with the sweetest of faces, skin like the top of a fatted weather rock, a woman his eyes had never met with before, but only his ears, during that of marvelous, fully decanted spouts.

When the time came that the dwarf could no longer sit idle by his starved desire, he began his journey to the fabled maiden. Unfortunately, the dwarf encountered struggle within his self-appointed quest but moments after its heroic foundation; he was unable to keep himself afloat, naturally unaided by the fact that he was not a proficient swimmer.

Fortunately, there came a fish, who so happened to have the hobby of pulling logs on its way to and from it's enquiries; this so happened to be one of those log pulling situations. On seeing the dwarf, the fish widened its gills at the prospect of aiding a distressed in need, and so offered the struggling stranger a moment of rest upon its own floating tree. Yet, the proud and stubborn dwarf declined the fish's goodwill and continued on with his gallant attempt, one without the piteous aid of a passerby. Though the fish thought the dwarf's request to be odd, and quite questionable, especially for a layman's fee, it respected said wishes and let the other be, remaining close by of coarse, as change of minds do happen some time or another, even by the most idiotic of sources, and also, primarily, so the fish could fulfill its wanton need of doing a good deed.

Next came a fisherman. But instead of laying eyes upon the struggling dwarf, who was in the midst of desperately grasping at the flighting and uninterested waters, like a fly upon a mule's backside, the man's attention was caught by the very fish who had offered the dwarf aid but moments earlier. Overjoyed by the prospect of a weighty dinner, the man dropped his loyal net into the waters and somewhat immediately caught hold of the fish.

The time soon came when the dwarf could no longer float but even a scant portion of himself above water, and so fell beneath its slippery grip, watching as the soon to be buttered fish struggled to escape the net of a most absolute apocalypse; with an inevitable pull and a cut from the log, the fish was taken by the hungry fisherman, while the dwarf fell further below, only but a forced tick worth left of breath.

Finally came another fish. It passed by the departing dwarf's face and hands, feet and thighs, and un-patiently watched, waiting: like the fisherman, it too was hungry.

Section IV

A REACTION OF SENSIBILITY

Hoping the girl had understood anything he had said, the storyteller grinned, bowed, then waited for his audience's verbal response. Annabella gave the relatives of this and that, essentially vocalizing how awful she felt for those in the story, and wished to change the happenings so that all obtained what she deduced was supposedly wanted (and so it was: The first fish was compelled, after being half-devoured and forced down the consequently fatal choking fisherman, to carry the drowned dwarf to the other side of the river, before itself expired, where the charlatan's empty eyes and nose, these being all the second fish had time to consume at the moment, met with those of the beautiful maiden across the water. And when the mistress was told of the dwarf's quest, she fell to the hunting ground sobbing, blaming herself for the death of another, wishing the same to fall upon herself for causing such shame. But after an extensive melancholic session, she felt upon the carcass's stomach something move, and fidget, until at last a bloodied fish gushed out from the dead dwarf in a spectacular manner, only to expire moments later with the fabled one as well).

The blue-lipped bell-clinking dunce, ignorant that the story had changed in reality, looked on at the girl as she smiled into a black hole of bliss. Naturally, he became annoyed by the one layered answer, and the fact that no matter what he said, nor how he said it, was to be interpreted, he thought, like an infantile page, one heavily inebriated by a tossed barrel of anquestian palm juice. But alas, the pompous intellectual was able to put his temperament aside for a moment, after sounding every bell and thingamabob upon his person, and so felt the sudden coolness that had taken throughout his toes during his time of storytelling: the coming of night had began its decent some time ago.

"I shall make a fire to relieve this unfortunate discomfort," announced the it, in a manner that voiced his innate fire making burden, one dictated within the precious inane masculine bestiaries of old; and thus a fire was built.

But when only embers remained, and laziness to fetch wood ruled, he looked desperately to every corner to satisfy himself, his instruments responding to each spark of his flame, while his cheeks hugged themselves together every chance he gave, he simply remained seated and sighed.

The beginning of the event filled the girl with the utmost of satisfactions; how wonderful it was to watch the warmth driven bran-crook enjoy himself. Yet, when only the settling glow of a once lively heat remained, she wished the gluttoning-clown to continue on with his merriment, one to grow and grow until he was as hot as could be and no longer in need of any fire or the desire to feel more warmth.

And so, as Annabella's ill fated attempt at sympathy spewed forth, so did the flames, surrounding and entrenching and becoming what was and was to be of the clown, until he could no longer feel but even a shadow of coolness upon the eyelash of a snowflake.

And so he burned.

Oh how he burned.

Section V

OF THE SNAKES

Perhaps you were expecting some sort of gypsy curse, or a harrowed verse to tickle your purse, but the mentioned character simply burned and burned, nothing more, nothing less.

It was not spectacular, nor was it underwhelming.

It was just right.

As there came to be but only ashes and dust within the centre of an empty pit, the girl looked on, hoping the ugly creature the best of hopes, and some wishes of clarity, truly oblivious to what the reader has possibly observed, as that may be whatever they may have deduced, her gaze forsood herself (i.e. veiled her understanding because of her innocence and inability to have accurate sympathy, and somewhat euphorically blinded by her own desires) until the moment came that a puddle of snakes, ones without heads or feet, were born from the powder-blankets of flesh left behind.

The hypnotically scaly, though not slimy, for whoever believes snakes are moist on the outside are completely delirious, self-employed harbingers waved their bodies in dry but methodical mannerisms, like broken damns giving way to a fortress of recluse but well hibernated bears.

"What kind of thing could be so ignorant to the minds of beasts," the snakes judged maliciously. "It is as if she listens to a cruel ocean wave, but cannot hear the squawks of the coming scavengers or the force of a most hideous destruction, but only the sweetened breath of fanciful ripples and its 'genuine' harmonies of trust."

The sapiens sung on in the most sapient of voices the following unnerving tune:

Things that could have been,
would have been,
should have been,
but never were,
nor will they ever be.
These are but the fabled tables of 'regret,'
flowered by the most delicate of edibles;
So forget not to eat,
even though their beauty and commonness
may blind you.

Without a moments hesitation, after, of coarse, the aforementioned still moment of appropriate observation, the slenders made their way around Annabella, rapping about every part they could possibly find, with each of their eyes playing their own sagacious, sardonic games, sucking between all the tender saplings for the syrup that lay inside themselves.

Though the girl felt most beyond 'horribleness,' 'destruction,' and 'worthlessness,' to say the least, she felt beyond the simple word of 'shame, and also a strange mis-worded sensation of 'embarrassment.' Yet, a shushed voice within herself spoke of '-----,' and that of '---------,' and so she felt 'confused' at the 'awkward' happening. She stayed as she was, stabbing at her desperate mind for an answer, but nothing came.

She was alone.

How Annabella wished to be anywhere else but where she was; her mind had left her to save her soul.

How she wished such a thing was possible.

Section VI

HATE

There are those who are blessed with the produce and harvests of life, taking whatever they deem to be their own, simply because a subjugating, privileged reasoning, one they may perhaps be aware of, or not; nevertheless, each pregnant situation is to be their own by right of proclamation, as her fate did decide, as all our patriarchs hum to the hymns of Adam's given rights, and the later's traitory within His manipulative, contorted garden.

And then there are those who are taken, a morality housed by profiting pathetics.

Though I desire, I will not press this story and dismissed ethics on much further, though it seems I am preparing myself for a heretical, decanting sermon, one that will never be heard, no matter what they may say, even though I and they have seen the devil within the man, the psychopath within the beast, the rapist and the thief, all of whom seem to win the clergy and laity by the heart strings, as if puppets within a wedding ring. And every time my mind passes from one "soul" to another, I simply meet another of the same making, disgusting, opportunistic, selfish, willing and wanting to take and make itself towards whatever it deems the moment's gold.

Section VII

LOVE

The girl of this story was of a different sort: She cared. Though her sympathy was confused: She hoped. Though her mind was in and of twixt, one of kindness, and another of obliviousness, one of happiness, and another of guilt: She loved.

If ever I had the choice, a moment of meeting another who tried to read my needs, but always misinterpreted, or a disinterested, self-consumed prude, I would chose the former in less than a moment's thought, as she the former is truly worth more than a countless life times, a woman who cares enough to try, and keep on, even when others place disheartening voices in her ear, telling her of many things, all until she does not even know what she wants, confused and wandering, and then finally rejecting whatever it was that she, at least he thought, was a part of what was worth continuing on.

But of coarse, Annabella chose the voices that pressed themselves most forcefully to her ear, as they seemed to be the ones to bring about more pressure and anxiety she wished to rid herself clear, at least he thinks, but does not.

And with each decision she made, she destroyed a past self; though if it was freely made, of that of which she wished upon herself, that is of another lifetimes philosophy, one which will forever scar my dreams.

So the girl breathed her last breath, after years of supposedly being pressed into a grave without bells, one she thought to be her home, a place she could perhaps live in after her world had forever changed, no longer a slave to a trusted familial aid.

But alas, I hope she finds what she is looking for.

I wish her all the happiness.

As I love her with all my heart, my mind, and my soul.

I hope she finds what she is looking for.

And for Annabella, once again she found herself below, as an Under-ling, somewhere underground.

Though, I believe, even if I wish to meet her apart from my dreams, I will never know.

The End

And goodbye.

that's it